W9-BFO-074

Young Cam Jansen

and the
Zoo Note Mystery

BY DAVID A. ADLER

ILLUSTRATED BY SUSANNA NATTI

PUFFIN BOOKS

For my great-niece,
Samantha Annabelle
—D. A.

To John Walker and Laura Kathryn Crenshaw
—S. N.

PUFFIN BOOKS
Published by Penguin Group
Penguin Young Readers Group,
345 Hudson Street, New York, New York 10014, U.S.A.
Penguin Books Ltd, 80 Strand, London WC2R ORL, England
Penguin Books Australia Ltd, 250 Camberwell Road, Camberwell, Victoria 3124, Australia
Penguin Books Canada Ltd, 10 Alcorn Avenue, Toronto, Ontario, Canada M4V 3B2
Penguin Books (N.Z.) Ltd, 182-190 Wairau Road, Auckland 10, New Zealand

First published in the United States of America by Viking,
a division of Penguin Putnam Books for Young Readers, 2003
Published by Puffin Books, a division of Penguin Young Readers Group, 2004

1   3   5   7   9   10   8   6   4   2

THE LIBRARY OF CONGRESS HAS CATALOGED THE VIKING EDITION AS FOLLOWS:
Adler, David A.
Young Cam Jansen & the zoo note mystery / by David A. Adler ; illustrated by Susanna Natti.
p.   cm.
Summary: Cam helps her friend Eric when he misplaces his permission slip to go on the school field trip.
ISBN: 0-670-03626-9 (hc)
[1. School field trips—Fiction. 2. Schools—Fiction. 3. Mystery and detective stories.]
I. Natti, Susanna, ill.   II. Title.   PZ7.A2615 Yj 2003 [E]—dc21 2002015553

Puffin Easy-to-Read ISBN 0-14-240204-4
Puffin® and Easy-to-Read® are registered trademarks of Penguin Group (USA) Inc.

Printed in China
Set in Bookman

Reading Level 2.0

CONTENTS

1. OH, NO!

"It's too bad you can't

go with us to the zoo,"

Cam Jansen said

to her friend Eric Shelton.

"Oh yes I can," Eric said.

"All last week

I forgot to bring the note.

But today I remembered."

Eric reached into his

right pants pocket.

He reached into his

left pants pocket.

"I wish I didn't always forget

where I put things," he said.

"I wish I had a memory like yours."

Cam has an amazing memory.

Cam says it's like a camera.

"I have pictures in my head," she says,

"of everything I've seen.

The camera in my head,

the one that takes

those pictures, goes click!"

"Here's the note," Eric said.

"It was in my shirt pocket."

Cam clicks

when she wants the camera

in her head to take a picture.

She also clicks

when she wants to remember something.

Cam's real name is Jennifer,

but because of her great memory

people called her "The Camera."

Soon "The Camera" became just "Cam."

"Look what else I brought," Eric said.

He opened his lunch box

and took out a sandwich.

"Cream cheese," Cam said.

"I don't like cream cheese.

It sticks to my teeth."

Eric took out a bag

of chocolate chip cookies.

"I know you like cookies.

I brought enough for both of us."

"Let's go, let's go,"

Mrs. Lane, the bus driver,

called to Cam and Eric.

"We're here. It's time to get off the bus."

Eric put everything back

and closed his lunch box.

It went click!

Cam and Eric hurried off the bus.

They went to their class.

They hung up their jackets

and sat in their seats.

"Good morning,"

their teacher, Ms. Dee, said.

"I remembered to bring

the note,"

Eric told her.

He reached into

his right pants pocket.

He reached into

his left pants pocket.

11

"But I can't find it," he said.

He reached into his shirt pocket.

"Oh, no," Eric said.

"The note is gone."

2. I'M REALLY SORRY

"I had it on the bus,"

Eric said.

"I really did.

My father signed it.

He said I could go

on the trip."

Cam told Ms. Dee,

"I saw it."

"I'm really sorry,"

Ms. Dee said to Eric.

"Without the signed note,

you can't go on the trip."

Eric checked his pockets again.

He didn't find the note.

"Check the hall,"

Ms. Dee said.

"Maybe the note fell out

on your way to class."

Cam and Eric checked the hall.

They found some papers,

but they didn't find

Eric's note.

Cam and Eric went to the office.

While they waited to ask

if someone had found the note,

Cam looked outside.

She saw their bus.

"That's it!" Cam said.

"You didn't drop the note

in the hall.

You dropped it in the bus.

Let's get outside

before the bus leaves."

3. IT'S COLD

When Cam and Eric got outside,

the bus was driving off.

"Stop! Stop!"

Cam and Eric shouted.

They waved their hands

and ran after the bus.

The bus stopped.

The door opened.

"Are you in trouble?"

Mrs. Lane asked.

"Have you been sent home?"

"No," Cam told her.

"Are you sick?"

"No," Eric said.

"I lost a note.

I think I lost it

on the bus."

"Oh," Mrs. Lane said.

"I'll help you look for it."

Cam and Eric got on the bus.

Cam, Eric, and Mrs. Lane

looked on the bus seats

and under them.

They didn't find the note.

They thanked Mrs. Lane.

They got off the bus.

"Now what do we do?"

Eric asked.

"We go inside," Cam said.

"It's cold out here."

As they walked,

Eric said, "That's because

we're not wearing our jackets."

Cam stopped.

"That's right," she said.

"We had jackets

when we came to school."

"And I had the note,"

Eric added.

"Yes," Cam said.

She thought for a moment.

Then Cam said,

"Maybe you *did* put the note

in your pocket.

Maybe you put it in your jacket pocket."

"And I know where my jacket is,"
Eric said.

"It's in our classroom.

Let's go."

4. CLICK! THAT'S IT!

Cam and Eric

hurried to their classroom.

"Did you find the note?"

Ms. Dee asked.

"No," Eric said,

"but I know where it is."

Cam and Eric went to the closet.

Eric reached

into the right pocket

of his jacket.

He reached

into the left pocket.

"It's not here," he said.

Eric sat in his seat.

"I can't find the note,

so I'm not going to the zoo."

"I'm sorry," Ms. Dee told him.

Ms. Dee spoke to the class

about the trip.

"We must stay together,"

she said.

"And I have to stay here,"

Eric whispered to Cam.

"I expect you to read the signs in the zoo,"

Ms. Dee said,

"and obey the rules."

Eric whispered,

"And I bet you expect me

to sit in the principal's office."

Eric turned to Cam and whispered,

"Cam, why don't you click?

Maybe that would help you

find my note."

Cam looked at Eric.

"Did you say, 'Click'?" she asked.

"Yes," Eric answered.

"I think *you* just solved

the mystery," Cam said.

"I think I know where to find your note."

5. A COOKIE FOR THE RIDE

"When you said 'Click,'"

Cam told Eric,

"I remembered

the last time you clicked."

"The last time I clicked?" Eric said.

"I don't click."

"You don't," Cam said,

"but your lunch box does.

On the bus

after you showed me the note,

you opened your lunch box.

You showed me your sandwich

and chocolate chip cookies.

Then Mrs. Lane told us

it was time to get off the bus.

You put everything back

and quickly closed your lunch box.

It clicked.

I think you put the note

in your lunch box.

Let's look."

Eric got his lunch box.

He opened it.

Cam found Eric's note.

It was under

the chocolate chip cookies.

"Hooray!" Eric said.

"Now I can go on the trip."

He gave the note

to Ms. Dee.

Ms. Dee told the class,

"Now we're *all* going on the trip."

Children in the class cheered.

Eric smiled.

"Now let's get ready,"

Ms. Dee told the class.

"It's a long ride to the zoo."

Cam and Eric put on their jackets.

They took their lunch boxes

and got in line.

"Here, Cam," Eric whispered

as they followed Ms. Dee.

"Here's a cookie for the ride."

Cam looked ahead at Ms. Dee.

She looked at the cookie

and whispered to Eric,

"Let's not wait for the ride."

Cam Jansen has an amazing memory. Do you?

Look at this picture. Blink your eyes and say, "Click!" Then turn to the next page.

A Cam Jansen
Memory Game

Take another look at the picture on page 31.

Study it.

Blink your eyes and say, "Click!"

Then turn back to this page

and answer these questions:

1. What color is Cam's jacket?

2. What color is Eric's jacket?

3. How many giraffes are in the picture?

4. Is Cam carrying her lunch box?

5. Is there a teddy bear in the picture?

6. Is anyone wearing a hat?